Junkyard Dan

Poison, Anyone?

NOX PRESS
books for that extra kick to give you more power
www.NoxPress.com

Also by Elise Leonard:

The **JUNKYARD DAN** series: (***Nox Press***)
1. Start of a New Dan
2. Dried Blood
3. Stolen?
4. Gun in the Back
5. Plans
6. Money for Nothing
7. Stuffed Animal
8. Poison, Anyone?
9. A Picture Tells a Thousand Dollars
10. Wrapped Up
11. Finished
12. Bloody Knife
13. Taking Names and Kicking Assets
14. Mercy

THE SMITH BROTHERS (a series): (***Nox Press***)
1. All for One
2. When in Rome
3. Get a Clue
4. The Hard Way

A LEEG OF HIS OWN (a series): (***Nox Press***)
1. Croaking Bullfrogs, Hidden Robbers
2. 20,000 LEEGS Under the C
3. Failure to Lunch
4. Hamlette

The **AL'S WORLD** series: (***Simon & Schuster***)
Book 1: Monday Morning Blitz
Book 2: Killer Lunch Lady
Book 3: Scared Stiff
Book 4: Monkey Business

Junkyard Dan

Poison, Anyone?

Elise Leonard

NOX PRESS
books for that extra kick to give you more power

www.NoxPress.com

Leonard, Elise
Junkyard Dan series / Poison, Anyone?
ISBN 978-1-935366-00-3

Copyright © 2008 by Elise Leonard.
All rights reserved, including the right of reproduction in whole or in part in any form. Published by Nox Press.
www.NoxPress.com

Printed in the U.S.A.
First Nox Press printing: November 2008
Second Nox Press printing: October 2009

books for that extra kick to give you more power

To all of us who are survivors:
whether it be of heartache,
or sickness,
or bad choices
or unfortunate events.
And for those of us who are *still* fighting the fight:
whether it be for literacy,
or health
or to save someone else.
Keep surviving, keep fighting,
and most importantly,
keep dreaming.

My thoughts are with you.

Many thanks to Jerry MacNeish,
owner of the cool Z28 on the cover.
He's a Camaro expert who has actually
"written the book" on old Camaros!

~Elise

Chapter 1

I came back in from burying the cat.

Lucky was by my side.

I went to the kitchen sink. To wash my hands.

"Seen a lot of loss?" I asked Lucky.

He looked up at me.

He didn't answer.

"I guess I've been lucky," I told the dog. "I haven't."

Lucky stared at me.

"You know," I said. "Seen a lot of loss."

I opened the fridge.

Lucky licked his lips.

He was now staring at the fridge. Well, the contents of the fridge.

"Hungry?" I asked him.

That was a stupid question.

The lady from the pound? She'd said that he'd been starved.

"How about a sandwich?" I asked him.

I didn't know if he understood me or not. But he licked his lips again.

"Roast beef okay with you?" I asked.

Lucky tilted his head.

He looked at me.

"Or do you want ham?" I asked him.

He barked. Twice.

It sort of sounded like *roast beef*.

"Roast beef it is, then," I told him.

He licked his lips again.

I didn't know if it was all in my head. But he seemed *really* smart.

I took out the roast beef.

Reached for the bread.

"You a ketchup dog? Or a mayo dog?" I asked him.

He didn't answer.

Poison, Anyone?

"Most people like ketchup. I like mayo."

He licked his lips again.

"I'll give you both," I told him. "So you'll know you're wanted here."

I swear he smiled at me.

"Just don't tell the other dogs. Okay?" I told him.

He squinted his eyes at me.

I swear he knew what I was saying.

"I can't afford to buy roast beef for everyone around here," I explained.

He was still squinting.

"Do you *know* how expensive roast beef is?" I asked him.

He licked his lips again as I smeared ketchup on the bread.

"It costs a lot more than dog food, Lucky."

He watched me spread mayo on the other slice of bread.

"So don't expect this," I told him. "It's a special treat. Your first meal here and all."

I think he nodded.

I took out some lettuce.

"Lettuce?" I offered.

He made a face.

I guess dogs don't do lettuce.

"No problem," I told him. "But I like the extra crunch."

Lucky waited patiently.

When I was done? I put mine on a plate.

I didn't know what to do with his.

So I just held it out to him.

I curled my fingers up so I wouldn't lose them.

Like when you feed a horse.

That's what you're supposed to do.

I read that somewhere. I don't think I've ever fed a horse. At least not that I can remember.

But I *do* remember reading that you should curl your fingers up. Underneath. You know. So you don't lose them.

I was shocked.

I expected Lucky to snap my hand off.

But he didn't.

He took the sandwich… almost politely.

Poison, Anyone?

He opened his mouth. His teeth were showing. But he took the sandwich gently.

Sure. He ate it in one bite.

It seemed like he'd swallowed it whole.

But he took it gently.

I felt sorry for him. Thinking about how someone had starved him.

So I took mine off the plate. Then I gave it to him.

He took that one gently as well.

Then he ate that one in one bite too.

He didn't seem to miss the ketchup. Not one bit. Hardly noticed the lettuce, too.

"Shall I make some more?" I asked him.

I think he smiled.

He ate two more. And I had two.

I didn't bother with the ketchup. He seemed fine with mayo.

"Okay, Lucky. Now we get to spackle and paint the walls in the office."

We went to the shed to look for supplies.

Chapter 2

After we brought supplies in? It was time to get to work.

I hadn't expected much help from Lucky.

He was just there for the company.

And I must admit, he was good company.

He just hung around and listened.

I was spackling the holes. The holes left by the pushpins Bubba had used. The pins in the maps. The maps that had helped find the person who owned the car. The car that had the kidnapped boy in it.

"I'm glad we found that boy," I told Lucky.

Lucky just looked at me.

"And I'm happy he was okay," I added.

Poison, Anyone?

I spread more spackle onto the wall.

"But his father? What a skunk!"

I looked at Lucky.

"Can you imagine that? Using your own kid? To con money? That's pretty low!"

Lucky whined a little.

As if he were agreeing with me.

"I guess you've had a few skunks in your life. Huh, Lucky?"

Lucky whined again.

"Well, at least one skunk. But he was a bad one. A really bad guy."

I looked at Lucky's oozing sores. They were healing a little. But they would take time.

Lucky's head jerked up.

He barked.

He'd heard something.

Just then, Miles poked his head in the office.

"I'm going to take off for a while," Miles said.

I turned around. "Okay, Miles."

"I'll catch you when I get back," he said.

I nodded. "Okay."

"Take care," he called as he left the room.

"You, too," I called to his back.

Lucky barked.

"'Bye, Lucky," Miles called over his shoulder. "Take care of the place while I'm gone."

Lucky barked again.

I know this will sound stupid. But I really do think Lucky understands English.

Miles closed the screen door with a slam.

I looked at Lucky.

"You're a good watchdog," I said.

I finished the spackle job.

Now I had to wait for it to dry.

After that? I could paint.

"So where do you think that poison came from?" I asked Lucky.

I'd taken the vial out from the car.

The car where we'd found the dead cat.

The cat had been chewing on the vial. So there was a hole in the top of the plastic cap.

I made sure I kept the vial upright.

I also made sure I washed my hands well. You

Poison, Anyone?

know, after I touched it.

For the rest of the day? I just hung around.

I watched some TV. Then I drove into town.

I stopped at Hilda's diner.

"Hey, Dan," Hilda called out.

"Hi, Hilda," I called back.

She was behind the counter.

"What's today's special?" I asked.

"I've got two," she answered.

I waited.

"I've got an enchilada plate," she said.

"What comes with that?" I asked.

"Some black beans and rice."

Wow. That sounded good.

"Or," she said.

She walked over and brought a glass of water.

"You can have the meatloaf."

"What comes with that?" I asked.

"Mashed potatoes and gravy. And those green beans you like."

"The ones with the little bits of bacon?" I asked.

"Those are the ones," she said with a cackle.

I thought about it.

I couldn't decide.

I wanted both.

"I can't decide," I told Hilda.

"Want both?" she asked.

I smiled. "It's like you read my mind."

"Want to start with the enchilada plate?" she asked.

"Sounds perfect!"

She went in the back to make my meal. Or should I say *meals*.

My mind wandered as I thought of that vial of poison.

Where did it come from?

Who made it?

Did they use it?

If so, why?

What did they use it for?

It killed a cat. Did it kill anything or anyone else?

What kind of poison was it?

Chapter 3

"Wow," Hilda said. "You look serious."

I was thinking so hard? I didn't even hear her come over to me.

"I was thinking," I said.

"About what?" she asked.

She set the enchilada plate before me.

It smelled great.

I looked around.

I was the only one there. The diner was empty.

It was between meal times.

"Can you sit with me?" I asked her.

"Sure," she said.

She hefted her body into the booth.

She sat across from me.

"So what's up?' she asked.

"We found a vial of poison. In a car," I explained.

"Poison?" she asked. "How do you know it's poison?"

"Well, we *think* it's poison," I said.

"Who's 'we'?" she asked.

"Bubba and me."

She laughed.

"You *do* realize that it could be anything. With Bubba guessing? For all you know? It could be perfume!" she said.

She cackled again.

I guess she didn't hear about the cat.

If she had? She wouldn't be laughing.

"We think it killed a cat," I told her.

She stopped laughing right away.

"Oh. Man. I'm sorry, Dan. I didn't know," she said.

I nodded. "It's okay."

Well, it was okay about her laughing. It was *not* okay about the cat.

Poison, Anyone?

"Was the cat one of yours?" she asked.

I nodded. "Yes."

"Oh," she said softly. "I'm so sorry."

I just nodded.

"Hopefully that's the last," she said.

I ate a bite of enchilada. It was great. I scooped up some beans and rice as well.

They, too, were great.

I finished chewing.

"The last of what?" I asked Hilda.

She made a face.

"I've always thought that bad things come in threes," she said.

"What?" I asked.

I didn't get what she was saying.

"Bad things," she repeated. "They always come in threes."

I took another bite of rice and beans.

Wow, they were good.

"Like what?" I asked.

"Like Jose Cruz passing. Then Rosa Cruz leaving to go home. Then your cat."

I thought about that. Those *were* three bad things.

I'd never met Jose, but his passing was sad.

I'd just met Rosa, and her leaving was sad.

And of course, my cat dying was bad, too.

I finished off the enchilada plate in no time.

"I love watching you eat," Hilda said. "It makes me feel good."

I had to laugh at that.

"Your food? It makes *me* feel good!" I told her.

"I like that you like my cooking so much," she said.

She cackled again.

"Ready for the meatloaf plate?" she asked.

I smiled. "I was born ready."

She pulled herself up from the booth.

She took the used, dirty enchilada plate.

Then she walked to the kitchen to get me the meatloaf plate.

When she came back she had two plates.

"Yum," I said. "I get two plates?"

Hilda cackled again.

Poison, Anyone?

"One is for me," she said. "I thought I'd join you."

"Oh," I said. "Okay."

She cracked up.

"Don't look so disappointed, Dan. If you want more? There's plenty more where that came from."

I just smiled.

Then I dug in.

The meatloaf was amazing. The potatoes? Light and fluffy. The gravy was smooth.

And the green beans?

Perfect.

"So where did the poison come from?" Hilda asked.

I dipped the meatloaf into the gravy.

"A car. It was wedged in the front seat."

"Do you know who owned the car?" she asked.

"Not yet," I said.

I ate some more mashed potatoes with gravy.

"But it's easy enough to find out."

Chapter 4

After a few pieces of pie? (A la mode, of course.) I was ready to go home.

"Thanks, Hilda," I said.

I patted my stomach.

"This should last me a little while."

Hilda laughed.

"I certainly hope so," she said.

"Maybe I should take an extra piece of apple pie home," I said. "You know, for later."

"I can wrap one up for you," she said. "You want me to?"

"Sure," I said. "Just add it to the bill."

"Okay," she said.

She went to the back.

Poison, Anyone?

She came out with a paper bag.

"Here you go, sir," she said.

She was grinning.

"Have ice cream at home?" she asked.

"Sure do," I said.

"Okay," she said. "Just checking. I know you like it with ice cream on top."

I smiled.

"Heat it up a bit before you eat it," she said.

I had to laugh.

"Stop it, Hilda. You're making me hungry again."

"How can you be hungry after eating all of that?!" she bellowed.

"You know I can't resist your apple pie!"

"You just had *two* pieces!" she screeched. "*And* a slice of blueberry!"

I shrugged.

"Hey. I like your cooking! Sue me!"

She was grinning from ear to ear.

I paid my bill. Then I left.

The ride home was hard.

I could smell that apple pie the whole way.

I would have eaten it in the car.

But I liked it with ice cream. And I didn't have any of that. Not in the car.

I'd *have* to wait until I got home.

I drove the car right up to the office.

I got out and took my paper bag.

I put the bag on the desk.

Then I went out to feed the animals.

When I was sure everyone had enough? I went back into the office.

I checked the walls.

The spackle was not dry yet.

So I decided to do some work.

I ran the VIN number on the car. The one with the poison.

I looked up the address.

It was about an hour away.

Too late to visit there today.

It was already late.

I would have called.

But I didn't want the owner to know that I was

Poison, Anyone?

coming.

Just in case.

In case they wanted to come up with a false story.

Or wanted to change their story.

Or were dangerous.

It was best to just show up and ask questions.

Without warning.

Like I'd done with that kidnapped boy's father. Earl.

His true colors sure did show right through!

This next guy? He could be a murderer!

I needed to catch this guy off guard.

But like I said. It was too late to go today.

Tomorrow was another day.

Chapter 5

The sun was shining brightly.

It looked like it would be a nice day.

I showered and shaved.

Then I pulled on some jeans. And a t-shirt.

I made some coffee, had some breakfast.

My spirits were up.

So much so, I wanted to call Rosa.

I just wanted to hear her voice.

I looked at the time.

She was probably at work already. So I called her office. The law firm.

It only rang twice.

"Rosa Cruz speaking," she answered.

All of a sudden? I was nervous.

Poison, Anyone?

A small wave of panic came over me.

"R-Rosa?" I stuttered.

"Yes," she said. I could tell she was distracted.

I heard papers rustling in the background.

"It's me. Dan," I said.

The papers stopped rustling.

"Dan," she said. "How wonderful to hear from you."

And you know what? She sounded really happy. Like it really *was* wonderful to hear from me.

That made me feel good. And made me less nervous.

"So how are you?" I asked.

"I'm good," she said.

Then she laughed.

"Okay," she said. "Maybe I'm not so good."

She started speaking quickly.

"I just miss Peaceville. I miss everyone there. I miss Mel and Henry. I miss Judge Simpkins. I miss Hilda's cooking. I miss… you."

She seemed a little nervous now.

I say that because after she said *that*? She started talking even faster.

"I even miss Bubba. Can you imaging that? I miss *Bubba*! How sad is it that I miss Bubba?! Right?"

I kind of heard the last thing she said. But I was more focused on that one sentence.

I miss... you.

Those words kept bouncing in my head.

I miss... you.

I miss... you.

I miss... you.

I mean, it *was* crazy that she missed Bubba.

He pestered her all the time. Always busted her chops.

But I really wasn't thinking of that.

I was only thinking of...

I miss... you.

I miss... you.

I miss... you.

Over and over.

"Right?" she said loudly.

Poison, Anyone?

I think she was still talking about how sad it was that she missed Bubba.

I *hoped* she was still talking about how sad it was that she missed Bubba.

Because to be honest? I hadn't really heard much since…

I miss… you.

"Right," I said.

She laughed. She sounded nervous. Unnerved.

I felt for her.

Knew how she felt.

I was nervous and unnerved too.

"So what are you up to?" she asked.

I told her about the teddy bear case.

"I wouldn't want to defend the father," she said. "That guy Earl is on his own."

"Yeah," I muttered.

"But the wife? I'd love to represent her for her divorce," Rosa said.

"If you lived here," I said softly.

"I'd also like to represent the parents," she said. "In a civil case against Earl."

"They probably won't press charges," I said.

She was quiet.

"I wasn't really trying to get them to," she said. "I was just thinking that maybe there *is* a need for a lawyer in Peaceville."

Oh. Now I got it.

Maybe she was looking for an excuse to come home.

A *real* excuse.

Something viable.

Something that would work out. A *reason* to come home.

"Oh. Right. Yes. You're right, Rosa. They *could* use a good lawyer to help them."

"Well," she said. "We'll see. I still don't know if there's enough business there. To support myself."

I wanted her to think about coming back. For selfish reasons, of course.

But I still wanted her to come back to Peaceville.

So I told her about what I was working on now.

Poison, Anyone?

She gasped. "*Poison*?" she choked out.

"We think so."

I told her about the cat.

"Where did it come from?" she asked.

"I'll be working on that today."

"Who put it there?" she questioned.

"I hope to find out."

"Why would it be there?" she asked.

"I don't know."

"Why would they *leave* it there?" she asked.

"I don't know that either," I replied.

"Hm," she said. "I wish I were there with you. I'd love to find out. Find out the answers to all of those questions."

I wished she were here with me too.

Just to be here with me. Not really to find out the answers to those questions.

I liked her company. Liked *her*. Liked having her around.

"I miss you too," I blurted out.

Then, in my head, I kicked myself.

It was stupid. I shouldn't have said it.

Why had I blurted that out?!

Couldn't I control my own mouth?

I felt like an idiot.

I'd said too much. Too much, too soon.

I heard her sigh softly.

"I miss you too, Dan," she whispered.

Wow. Those five words? They shot right through me.

On the one hand? I was thrilled.

On the other? A little scared.

Afraid to make another mistake.

Afraid to open myself up to someone.

I'd already made one mistake in my life. *If* you can call it that.

I'd loved Patti. With everything I had.

But that hadn't been enough for Patti.

Thoughts of Patti? They made me skittish. They spooked me.

Plus, they reminded me that in a way? I was still married

"I've got to go," I told Rosa sadly.

Chapter 6

"Okay, Dan," she said.

She sounded disappointed.

I was disappointed too.

My emotions were all over the place.

I didn't like that feeling.

But you want to know what? I didn't like the thought of her *not* in my life, either.

I'd have to work these feelings out.

But not now. I was too busy now.

Now? I had to deal with the poison problem.

"I'll call you soon," I said to Rosa. "Okay?"

"Okay, Dan," she said softly. Sweetly.

As I hung up the phone? My heart ached a little.

I wondered if hers did too.

I looked at the phone. The call was over.

It was time to get to work.

I took out the address for the last owner of the car. The car that had the poison in it.

I looked up directions to get there.

Then I wrote them down.

"Ready or not?" I said aloud. "Here I come."

* * *

The drive was nice. I liked driving in Florida. The air smelled good.

It was warm and a bit salty.

I even had to go over a long bridge.

The water sparkled in the sunlight.

It looked like diamonds were thrown all over the place.

I put on my shades. Turned up the music.

I opened all the windows.

My hair was whipping all over the place.

It felt great.

Poison, Anyone?

Like I was truly alive.

I breathed in deeply.

The car sped across the bridge. Hardly anyone was on the road.

I missed rush hour traffic by a couple of hours.

I thought about how I used to get stuck in city traffic in New York.

It was not fun. Take my word for it.

But this? This *was* fun.

At the moment? Life was good.

I think I learned something these last few months.

What did I learn?

Life is largely about the journey.

I used to think life was about the destination.

You know. Making my goal. Getting there. Arriving.

It *used* to be like that for me.

But lately? It's all about the journey.

The steps along the way.

Enjoying the ride.

Noticing the ride!

It may not sound like much.

But it's what I've learned lately.

And you know what?

I think my life would have been *very* different if I had thought that way before.

Chapter 7

I got to the house.

I checked the address twice.

Then a third time.

I don't know what I was expecting.

But it sure wasn't what I got.

The house was old. But well cared for.

It looked like a gingerbread house.

Everything just so.

Like a doll house.

Not a house a killer would live in!

I didn't know what a killer's house would look like. But it wasn't this.

This looked like it should be on the cover of a magazine. The Christmas issue. Of a cooking magazine.

Or a lady's magazine.

One with a gingerbread house on it.

A prize-winner.

With colored gum drops and licorice. And frosting all over it.

I checked the address once more.

It was correct.

So I knocked on the door.

No answer.

I rang the doorbell.

"Hello?" I called out.

Still no answer.

I rang again.

"Anyone home?" I asked loudly.

I heard someone walking toward the door.

They weren't running. But they weren't dawdling either.

"I'm coming," a small voice called out. "Keep your britches on."

That made me smile.

I hadn't heard that expression in a long time.

Poison, Anyone?

When I was a boy? My grandfather used it.

He used to always tell me to keep my britches on.

He used to say that I did things too fast.

While I waited for the lady to come to the door? I thought about that.

My grandfather was probably right.

I *did* do things too quickly.

When I was younger? I hadn't taken the time. The time to enjoy what I was doing. Or eating.

Or anything, really.

I was always in a big rush.

It was only now that I was seeing things differently.

It was only now that I was taking the time to slow things down. To see the big picture.

To enjoy things fully.

Like a car ride on a sunny day.

Like Hilda's pie.

Like the sound of someone's voice. (Okay, *Rosa's* voice.)

I was thinking about those things when the

person finally opened the door.

I hadn't expected the house.

That was a surprise.

But I also wasn't expecting the person who answered the door!

She was tiny. And old.

A little old lady.

She didn't look like a killer.

She didn't look scary at all!

She looked… harmless.

Chapter 8

"Hello," she said with a smile. "May I help you?"

"Yes," I said. "I'm looking for a man. The owner of an old Z28."

She looked at me and grinned.

Maybe she was a little senile.

"Do you know what I'm talking about?" I asked her.

"I think so," she said mildly.

"I'm talking about a car," I said.

She just kept looking at me. Smiling.

"A red car," I added.

Still smiling.

"Did you know anyone who had a red car?" I

asked her.

She stepped back a little.

"Would you like to come in?" she asked.

She was very polite.

Quite civil.

"Um," I said. I didn't know if I was wasting my time. I didn't think this old woman could help.

Didn't know if she would know about the car.

She was nice and all.

But she seemed a little… off.

Not crazy. Just… off.

She was still grinning.

"Please," she said. "Please come in."

Well, I *had* driven all the way there.

I stepped into her house.

The inside was as pristine as the outside.

Everything was in its proper place.

All of her stuff? It was old, but well made.

They don't make things like they used to. That's for sure!

Everything was an antique.

I passed through the hallway.

Poison, Anyone?

There was a small writing table against the wall.

It had all sorts of carvings on it.

Carvings that were *supposed* to be there.

Not graffiti.

I pointed to the writing table.

"That's very nice," I told her.

"Thank you," she said. "It was my mother's."

She laughed.

"I know what you're thinking," she said. "You're thinking, 'Wow, it must be old!'"

I didn't want to insult her.

"No. No," I said. "I wasn't thinking that."

"Sure you were," she said. "And you would be right!"

She laughed again.

"That old desk? It's older than dirt," she said with a chuckle.

Then she laughed again.

"After all," she said with a small wink. "*I'm* almost as old as dirt."

I wouldn't have put it quite that way.

But she *was* old.

"May I offer you some tea?" she asked.

Then she clutched her chest.

"Oh, foolish me," she said. "I don't even know who you are."

She looked at me head on.

"Who *are* you?" she asked.

I held out my hand. "I'm Dan. Dan Corbett. I own a junkyard. In Peaceville."

She looked off in the distance.

"I know Peaceville," she said. "It's a tiny little town. Nice people there."

"Yes, ma'am," I said.

"Kind of a one horse town. Like the old days," she said.

"Yes, ma'am," I agreed.

"A nice place. Is it still untouched?" she asked.

"Excuse me?" I said.

"You know. Untouched. Before the Wal-Marts and the Jiffy Lubes and the Starbucks came. Came and took over towns."

That made me laugh.

Poison, Anyone?

"No, ma'am," I said. "Peaceville does not have a Wal-Mart, a Jiffy Lube or a Starbucks."

"Good. Good," she said. "Those places? They make towns all look alike."

She had a point.

"You go to any town nowadays? They all look alike. They all have a Wal-Mart, a Jiffy Lube and a Starbucks."

I smiled.

"You could be anywhere," she said.

She tsked a few times and shook her head.

"Well, Peaceville is still, as you say, untouched," I told her.

"I'll have to go back there one day. To visit," she said.

"We'd love to have you," I told her. And I meant it.

"There was a diner there. A young woman. That young thing could cook!" she said.

I thought of Hilda's diner.

Hilda was no longer young. But maybe it was still her.

"Was the young cook's name Hilda?" I asked.

She thought about that.

"You know? I think it was!" she said. "I remember the young woman well. She was a sturdy thing. Built solid. But boy, that girl could *cook*."

I pictured Hilda. Yes, she would have been "sturdy" when she was younger. She also would have been "solid."

"She had this strange laugh," the woman said. "Like the witch from the Wizard of Oz."

"You mean like a cackle?" I asked.

The old lady laughed.

"Yes. That's it. Like a cackle."

I smiled. "That was Hilda!" I said.

"Is she still around?" the lady asked.

"Yes," I said. "And she cooks just as well now. Probably even better. She's the best cook I've ever come across."

The woman nodded.

"Yes. I'll have to go back there one day," she said. "But I don't drive any more. It's not really

Poison, Anyone?

safe. I'm too old."

I felt sorry for her.

The poor old thing had to give up her independence.

She seemed like she'd been a spunky thing. When she was younger.

"Does anyone else live here?" I asked her.

I looked around.

"No," she said. "It's only me. I'm the only one left."

It seemed a lonely life. And for a split second I lost my mind.

"Want to go there now?" I asked her.

She clapped her hands with glee.

"Oh really?" she asked.

Her old face lit up.

Her smile creased her whole face. Her eyes. Her cheeks. Her mouth.

All of a sudden? I was into the idea.

It sure made *her* happy.

"Yes," I said. "Really."

"That would be delightful," she said.

Chapter 9

She got her purse.

It looked just like a little old lady purse.

She snapped it shut and smiled.

"This will be nice, Mr. Corbett. Thank you."

I wondered if this was a good idea.

It seemed as if it were. At the time I offered.

But now? Not so much.

"Are you sure you want to take this trip?" I asked her.

She nodded.

"Quite sure."

"It's a long ride," I said.

"That's okay," she said with a grin. "I'm a lot tougher than I look, Mr. Corbett."

Poison, Anyone?

"Please," I said. "Call me Dan."

She smiled.

"And you may call me Violet."

"Pleasure to meet you, Violet," I said to her.

"The pleasure is all mine, Dan. The pleasure is all mine."

We left the house and she locked the front door.

She slipped her keys in her purse. Then snapped it shut again.

I helped her down the front steps.

She took my arm. But I could tell that she really didn't need my help.

It seemed she *was* a lot tougher than she looked.

She looked frail. Fragile. But she really wasn't.

We walked to my car.

I opened her door, and helped her into the car.

Then I walked to the driver's side and got in.

"I like your car," she said.

"Thank you," I replied.

I didn't turn on the radio.

The last station I'd had on? Rock.

Loud, churning, blaring rock.

The station played rock and hip hop. And I didn't think she'd approve.

Or enjoy it.

So I kept the radio off.

I did turn on the AC.

But kept it low.

I didn't want to blow her out of the car.

Or freeze the poor woman.

She sat quietly.

Looking out the windows.

We didn't talk much.

I could tell she was enjoying the ride.

"It's been a while since I've done this," she said.

I smiled.

"What? Run off with a stranger?" I asked.

She giggled.

She actually giggled.

"Yes," she said. "There's that. But I'd meant that it has been while since I went joyriding."

Poison, Anyone?

Ha. *Joyriding*. That was funny.

She was a quirky old thing.

Old on the outside. But she seemed young on the inside.

I hoped I'd age that way.

If you thought about it? It was kind of cool.

We got to the bridge. The long bridge.

The water was still sparkling in the sunlight.

She touched my arm.

"Mind if we open the windows?" she asked. "Get some air in here?"

I remembered the ride to her house.

"It'll get pretty windy," I said.

She smiled. "I don't mind."

I looked at her perfectly curled blue hair.

"Your hair will get ruined," I said.

She smiled widely.

"To heck with that. Let's throw caution to the wind," she said.

I had to smile.

"Are you sure, Violet?"

"Positive."

I turned off the AC and lowered the windows.

Violet laughed and laughed.

I watched as the wind whipped her hair into a frenzy.

Then she reached for the radio knob.

"You mind?" she asked me.

"I don't. But you might," I replied.

She pushed it in, and the radio blasted on.

Hip hop was roaring loudly.

I looked over at her.

She started bobbing her head to the beat.

"I love this song," she shouted over the music. "Don't you?"

"You like Lil Wayne?" I shouted back.

"Sure. Don't you?" she hollered back.

I nodded.

"He *could* clean up the lyrics a little bit, though," she said. "Don't you think?"

That made me smile.

It was more like something I thought she'd say.

But it was still way off.

I laughed at the thought. Little Miss Violet

Poison, Anyone?

listening to Lil Wayne.

That was funny.

"I can't believe that Beyoncé married Jay-Z. Can you?" she asked me.

I shrugged.

"I never thought about it."

"Do you think it'll last?" she asked.

This was the weirdest conversation I'd ever had.

"I never thought about it," I repeated.

Violet sure was a surprise a minute.

Chapter 10

The rest of the drive back to Peaceville was fun.

Yes, that's right.

I was sitting with a little old lady. A *blue haired* little old lady. And I was having fun.

She sure was unique.

I'd never met anyone like her.

We were in town now. Driving through. To get to the diner.

"Peaceville hasn't changed at *all*," she said.

"When was the last time you were here?" I asked.

"About thirty years ago," she said.

"Wow," I said. "And nothing has changed?"

Poison, Anyone?

She looked around.

"Nothing."

We got to the diner.

As usual? I parked right out front.

I got out and walked to Violet's side.

I opened the door and helped her out.

She touched her hair.

"I must look a mess," she said.

I looked her straight in the eye.

"You look beautiful," I told her.

For the second time that day, she giggled.

The sound made me laugh.

I know this will sound funny. But…

It also made my heart laugh.

It was then that I opened the door to the diner.

Hilda heard us come in.

"Hi Dan," Hilda called from the counter.

"Hey, Hilda," I said. "I'd like you to meet Violet."

Violet moved out from behind me.

Hilda laughed.

"I didn't see you come in. Dan was blocking

you," Hilda said with a laugh.

Hilda strode over to meet us.

I watched as Violet and Hilda shook hands.

Violet looked at Hilda. Then she looked at me.

"Yes, Dan. I think this is the same woman. The same woman who was here last time I was here."

I smiled at Hilda.

"Violet says your cooking was just as good years ago. When you were younger," I told Hilda.

"When were you last here?" Hilda asked Violet.

"About thirty years ago," Violet said.

Hilda smiled. "I'd just opened up then."

Then she looked at me.

"I mean. I *meant* to say, I wasn't even *born* then!" she said with a huff.

We all laughed.

"Well, honey," Violet said. "If your cooking is *anywhere* near as good as that young whipper-snapper's? It's a *treat* for me to be here today!"

Hilda beamed.

Then she winked at Violet.

Poison, Anyone?

"I'll see what I can do," was all Hilda said.

She then showed us to a booth.

My booth.

My usual booth.

"So what's the…" I started to ask.

Hilda cut me off.

"I know, I know. You want to know today's special," she said. "What else is new?"

We all laughed again.

Chapter 11

As we waited for our meals, we talked.

"Now what was it you drove all that way to ask me?" Violet asked.

"It was about a car," I said. "But I don't think you'll know about it."

She tried to look innocent. "You mean a *red* car?"

I nodded.

"That's right," I said.

She grinned slyly.

"A red Z-28? Muscle car? Two door? With a black roof? Black racing stripes? Chrome wheels? And black leather interior?"

I stared at Violet.

Poison, Anyone?

"*That* red car?" she asked.

I was afraid to ask.

She was such a surprise a minute.

"You know it?" I asked.

"Know it? I *owned* it," she replied.

I thought she was pulling my leg.

"For real?" I asked her.

She nodded her little blue head.

"For real."

"Did anyone else drive it?" I asked her.

She scoffed. "Are you *kidding*?! Did you *see* that baby? No one touched it but me."

That made me laugh.

"Are you sure you're the only one who owned that car?" I asked again.

"Yes," she answered.

"Did anyone else drive it? *Anyone*?" I asked her.

She thought about it.

"Well, maybe my granddaughter. Every now and then," she said quietly.

That was who I needed to speak with.

I had a strong feeling that Violet knew nothing of the vial. The vial of poison.

Just then, Hilda arrived with the food.

She placed my stuffed pork chops down first.

Then she placed Violet's turkey plate in front of her.

I looked at Violet's plate.

"That looks good," I told Hilda. "Now I wish I'd ordered that."

Hilda rolled her eyes.

"Okay. I'll make you one," she said with a sigh.

Then she reached to take my plate back.

"Hey. I never said that I didn't want this one too," I told her.

Hilda shook her head and cackled.

"I love your appetite, Dan," Hilda said.

Then she turned to go back to the kitchen.

"Yes," Violet said. "That's her. The cook from way back when. That laugh? It's hard to forget."

I nodded.

"Yes, it's unique," I agreed.

Poison, Anyone?

I needed to get back to the poison problem.

I cut into my pork chops and tasted them.

They were amazing, as expected.

I think I moaned with pleasure.

"How are your pork chops?" Violet asked.

"Fantastic," I said.

"Can I try some?" she asked.

I didn't like sharing my food. But this was an old lady. How could I say no?

"Oh, okay," I said.

I cut off a small chunk and put it on her plate.

"How's your turkey dinner?" I asked her.

"Perfect," she said.

"Can I try some?" I asked her.

She looked me square in the eye.

"No! You've got a whole *plate* of it coming to you!" she said with vigor.

I was a bit shocked.

But again, I thought that this old woman was *nothing* like I'd expected.

She sure was full of zip!

Chapter 12

"Mmm. You're right. This pork chop is great," Violet said.

I threw her a dirty look.

She laughed. "If you want a bit of my turkey? Okay. I'll give it to you. Just stop making those faces at me," she said.

I had to smile.

"It's not like I'm eating and you're starving," she said.

Hilda chose that moment to come to the table.

She set the turkey plate next to my pork chop plate.

"Forget it now," I told Violet. "It's too late."

She shook her head.

Poison, Anyone?

"No. I said I would. So I will," she said.

She cut off a bite-sized piece of turkey. Then she tossed it on my plate.

"There you go," she said. "Take food from an old lady."

Hilda hadn't been around for the teasing. The playfulness.

She didn't know Violet was joking.

"Dan!" Hilda scolded. "You're taking food from Violet's plate?!"

Hilda scowled at me.

"You should be ashamed of yourself, Dan Corbett!" Hilda yelled.

Hilda turned to Violet.

"I'll go get you some more, dear," she said to Violet.

Then Hilda turned to me again.

"Ashamed, Dan Corbett. Ashamed," she muttered as she went back to the kitchen.

Violet was grinning.

"See? Now *I'm* getting more too," she said to me.

"You're a strange old bird," I said with a wide smile. "But I like you."

She smiled back.

"Hey, I can eat well, too, you know. You're not the *only* one with a big appetite," she said simply.

She was a surprise a minute.

"You're picking up the tab for this. Right?" she asked.

She was trying to look innocent.

I had to laugh.

"Right."

"What about dessert?" she asked.

"What about it?" I asked back.

"You think I can get both the apple pie *and* the peach?" she asked me.

She was a woman after my own heart.

"Sounds like a plan to me," I said.

She grinned.

"You know what?" she asked.

"What?" I asked her.

"I like you too, Dan Corbett."

We sat there smiling at each other.

Poison, Anyone?

"So how can I get a hold of your granddaughter?" I asked her.

Violet's smile faded quickly.

Her eyes started to well up.

She tried to answer. But had to wait a few moments before she could speak.

"That's not going to be easy," was all she said.

Chapter 13

"Are you okay?" I asked Violet.

She tried to get a hold of herself.

She failed.

She was very upset by something.

Something about her granddaughter.

"It's still hard for me to deal with," she whispered.

I didn't know what to say.

Things were going so well.

We were having fun.

Everything was great.

Now things were strained.

But then again. We *were* talking about a vial of poison.

Poison, Anyone?

What did I expect?

I didn't want to push her.

I wanted to give her some time.

I was thankful when Bubba came into the diner.

"Hey, Dan," Bubba said.

"Hey, Bubba," I returned.

Then Bubba caught sight of Violet's face.

She still looked stricken.

I felt so bad. Like it was all my fault.

"Am I interrupting something?" Bubba asked.

I looked at Violet.

She wiped away a little tear.

"Oh, no. No. Please," she said. "Join us."

I looked at Violet.

"You may regret that," I said to her.

Bubba was pure Bubba.

I say that because of his next comment.

"Yeah. Dan likes to hog up all the cute chicks," he said.

Violet giggled.

I was glad to hear that sound again.

I looked up at Bubba and smiled.

"Yeah," Bubba went on. "If there's a hot chick around? Dan's always snapping her up."

He looked at Violet.

"I can see Dan's done the same thing here. Again!" he finished.

Bubba looked forlorn.

As if he'd missed out on his chance.

"Sonny?" Violet said to Bubba with a wink. "Don't you fret. You still have a shot with me."

At that, Bubba threw back his head and let out a loud "Yee Ha!"

Then he turned to me and smiled.

"I've still got it, cowboy!" he said to me.

Violet grinned from ear to ear.

"Why yes, you do," she said to Bubba coyly.

These two were a match made in heaven.

"Want to join us for dessert?" I asked Bubba.

"You payin'?" he asked.

I rolled my eyes.

"I guess so," I replied.

"Then it looks like I will," he said.

He winked at Violet.

Poison, Anyone?

She winked back at him.

"Dan said I could get two slices of pie," she told Bubba.

Bubba looked at me.

"Well as your guest? I expect nothing less than what *she's* getting," he said to me.

I rolled my eyes again.

"Whatever."

Bubba stuck his hand out.

"I'm Bubba."

Violet took his hand and shook it.

"Violet," she said.

"Like the flower," Bubba flirted.

"Like my hair color," she threw back at him.

We all laughed.

I was glad Bubba had arrived.

He'd gotten things back. Back to the way they were at first.

Without tears.

Hilda showed up with the pie after that.

Chapter 14

"Hey, Dan," Bubba said as we shoved pie in our pie holes.

I was afraid to ask.

Bubba had that look.

The one that meant I was not going to like what he had to say.

"What?" I asked slowly.

"I needed to get a part from the yard," he said. "I left the money for you in your desk drawer."

That was it?

I could deal with that.

That wasn't bad.

In fact? That was good.

A sale. Yay.

Poison, Anyone?

"Okay," I said. "Thanks."

"Yeah, well. When I got that part out?" he said.

Oh no. Here it comes.

I could feel it.

I was *not* going to like what he had to say next.

"Yes?" I asked slowly.

"I found a little card thingie," he said.

"A what?"

"One of those little card thingies. The kind you put in a camera. For pictures," he said.

Oh. That couldn't be bad.

It probably had pictures of someone's birthday.

Or their kid.

Or something else good.

Right?

All I had to do was track them down and return it.

They'd probably be happy about getting it back.

Right?

"I stuck it in your computer. You know. In those slots for the cards?" Bubba said.

"And?" I asked.

"And, let's just say…"

Bubba didn't know how to word the rest of the sentence.

That was not good.

If Bubba couldn't say it?

It had to be bad.

Very bad.

Very, *very* bad!

Oh, God. Here we go again.

"Can we discuss this later?" I asked Bubba.

Bubba looked at Violet.

"Yeah," he said. "Let's."

Oh, dang. This had to be really bad.

Great.

"More coffee?" Hilda asked.

She was standing beside the booth with a whole pot.

Coffee went so well with pie a la mode.

"Sure," I said. "I'd love some, Hilda."

"Me too," Violet said. "It's delicious."

"Me three," Bubba said. "Pour it in, gorgeous!"

Poison, Anyone?

Hilda gave Bubba a look.

"Don't try to flirt your way into not paying your check, Bubba. That doesn't work with me," Hilda said to Bubba.

"Dan's paying," Bubba said with a smile.

"You sure do spread it around, some. Don't you, Bubba," Violet said to Bubba.

"Don't worry, ladies. I've got plenty to go around," Bubba said with a grin.

I had to put my two cents in.

"Yes, he's got so much of it?" I told Violet. "You can dig it up and move it around with a shovel!"

Hilda cackled.

"Good one, Dan!" she said. "You're getting better with the cracks."

Bubba tried to look upset.

"That's your opinion," Bubba said to Hilda.

We all laughed.

Bubba too.

"Well," I said to Violet. "We should get going. It'll get dark soon. And we have a long ride back to your house."

"Yeah," Bubba said. "And I have to eat dinner. What are the specials?" Bubba asked Hilda.

"You just had two pieces of pie," Hilda said to Bubba.

"That was dessert. And Dan was paying. Now I need dinner."

Violet giggled again.

"It sure is fun around here," Violet said.

"Yeah," Hilda said. She threw Bubba a dirty look. "It's a laugh a minute."

We got up and I paid the bill on our way out.

I tried to leave Hilda a big tip. But she never let me.

"You forgot your change again, Dan," she hollered.

I had to walk back and get it from her.

"Would you stop doing that?!" Hilda hissed at me.

"Would you just take the tip you deserve?!" I hissed back.

Chapter 15

I put Violet into the car.

Then we took off for the highway.

"Thank you, Dan," she said strongly.

"No problem," I told her.

"This was the nicest day I've had in a long time."

That made me smile.

"I'm glad I could share it with you," I said. "It was a nice day for me too."

The sun was going down.

We saw the sun set over the water.

It was really quite beautiful.

"Want the radio on?" I asked her.

"No. It's nice to have quiet company," she said.

I knew what she meant.

I was alone a lot now.

And I missed that.

The quiet company of someone else.

Patti was rarely quiet. But at least she was company.

Now? Now I had no one.

Darkness was setting in.

I liked the darkness.

It's funny how you can say things in the dark that you'd never say in the daylight.

"I used to be married," I said aloud.

"Me too," she said softly.

The car sped along the highway.

"Sometimes I miss it," I said.

"Me too," she agreed.

We sat for a few minutes. Each with our own thoughts.

"Were you married long?" I asked her.

"Yes," she said. "A long time. Long enough to know what I'm missing now."

"So you had a good marriage," I commented.

Poison, Anyone?

"Yes," she said. "I was lucky. I married a good man."

She sighed softly after saying that.

I guess she missed her husband.

"The Lord took him way too soon," she whispered.

I didn't know what to say.

"Did you have a good marriage?" she asked me.

I shrugged.

"I thought I did," I said slowly.

"Until you didn't," she added.

I nodded. "That's right. Until I didn't."

"What went wrong?" she asked.

"I don't really know," I answered.

"You never asked her?" Violet asked.

"I never had time to ask," I explained. "My wife ran off with someone else."

"And you didn't know she was unhappy?"

"Not a clue," I said softly.

"Do you think she left you clues? But maybe you didn't see them?" she asked gently.

I thought about that.

"I put a lot of thought into things after Patti left me. I retraced our talks. Our nights. Our time spent together," I said.

"And?" she asked.

"And, I came up with nothing. For the life of me? I have no idea why my wife left me."

"You said she ran off?"

"Yes. She ran off with the 23-year-old roofer I'd hired to fix our roof," I explained.

"Hm," Violet said.

"She took everything. Everything that wasn't nailed down. Cleaned out all the bank accounts too. All but one small one she didn't know about."

"She sounds awful," Violet said. "Selfish."

I nodded. "That she was."

"So perhaps her leaving had nothing to do with you," Violet said simply.

"Perhaps."

"Perhaps it had everything to do with her. And nothing to do with you," she said boldly.

"Perhaps," I said.

Poison, Anyone?

Violet sat quietly.

"But it still hurt," I said.

There was a little light from the dashboard. And in that little light I could see Violet nod her petite head.

"Yes," she said. "I'm not a stranger to pain either."

Chapter 16

For the rest of the trip? We each sat with our own thoughts.

I didn't know about Violet. But for me? My thoughts ran wild.

I let them flow freely.

Thoughts of pain.

Thoughts of loss.

Thoughts of confusion.

When we got to Violets house? I was quiet and thoughtful.

Violet unlocked her front door.

She switched on the lights inside.

We stepped inside.

"May I get you anything?" she asked.

Poison, Anyone?

"No thanks. I should get going," I replied.

"Would you please stay?" she asked quietly. "At least for a little while?"

She looked lonely. Lost.

"Okay," I said. "If I'm not bothering you."

"No," she said. "You're not a bother. You're nice to have around."

I nodded quickly. "Thank you."

She showed me to a couch.

"Please," she said. "Sit down."

I sat down.

She sat next to me. She folded her hands and put them in her lap.

"You wanted to know about my granddaughter," she said.

"Yes."

She nodded tersely.

"A mother shouldn't outlive her child," she said softly.

I had to agree.

"But I still had my granddaughter," she said.

I had no idea what she was talking about.

She looked so tired. And all of a sudden she looked very old.

Don't get me wrong. She'd looked old before.

But now? Now she looked drawn. Drawn and haggard.

As if her memories wore her down.

Ate at her.

"A grandmother shouldn't outlive her grandchild," she whispered.

Her body crumpled.

I moved closer to her.

Felt the need to hold her. Comfort her.

My heart went out to this small woman.

"But I did," she said softly.

She looked up at me.

Tears filled her eyes.

"It's not right," she said more boldly.

I shook my head.

"No, it's not," I agreed.

The woman broke down and cried.

"My daughter? She married a bad man. A mean man. A selfish man."

Poison, Anyone?

She sobbed quietly.

"My daughter died of lung cancer. A long, horrible, painful death."

"I'm sorry," I mumbled.

And I was.

Violet nodded and smiled sadly.

Then she snorted a laugh.

"The funny thing was? She didn't even smoke."

She looked at me head on.

"*He* did," she said. "Her selfish husband smoked like a chimney."

I think I grimaced. But I wasn't sure.

"My granddaughter knew. She knew her father took away her mother."

Violet looked so sad. So broken.

She spoke without emotion.

"She hated her father. Hated him for causing the death of her mother."

I could relate to the child.

"My son-in-law wouldn't put up with her emotions. And like the selfish man he was? He left."

I was shocked by that.

"How old was the child?" I asked.

"Thirteen."

I sighed heavily.

"That's a rough time for a kid. Even without all those extra problems," I said softly.

"You've got *that* right," Violet agreed.

I wondered what happened next.

I didn't have to wonder for long.

"She called me after three days of being alone."

I choked with shock.

"Three days?!" I sputtered.

"Yes," Violet said. "She was alone and scared."

"I would imagine so," I replied.

"So I picked her up. Gathered her things. Brought her home here. And never took her back there."

"Good for you," I said.

She smiled sadly.

"It was awful for that poor child. All her stuff. In big black plastic garbage bags. She deserved

Poison, Anyone?

better."

Violet shook her head.

"Seems to me as if she *got* better," I said. "In *you*."

I gave her a little squeeze.

Her smile brightened slightly. "Thank you, Dan."

I gave her a few minutes with her thoughts.

Finally I asked.

"Did she die of lung cancer too?"

Violet's eyes filled with tears.

"That's the saddest part of all," she whispered.

She stood up. Then she smoothed the front of her dress.

"May I offer you some tea?" she asked me.

"No thank you."

"Coffee?"

"No thank you," I said evenly.

"A cold drink?" she asked.

"No, I'm fine," I told her. "Thank you."

I could tell she wanted something to do. *Needed* something to do.

Chapter 17

"Please, Violet," I said. "Sit and talk to me."

She sat back down.

Leaned into me.

She felt so frail. So lost.

"Why are you here?" she asked.

I thought the best thing for her was to tell the truth.

"We found a vial in your car. A vial of poison."

Violet gasped. "Poison?"

"Yes. It killed one of my cats. In my junkyard."

"How?" she asked.

"The cat bit a hole in the top of the vial. We found her dead."

Violet gasped again.

Poison, Anyone?

"It must be from my husband's work," she said softly.

I was confused.

"Your husband worked with poison?"

She shook her head.

"He was a scientist. A researcher."

That hadn't cleared things up for me.

Then she gasped again.

"Oh please," she cried out. "No!"

"What?" I asked her.

She looked up at me. Her eyes looked frantic.

"My husband had died right before my daughter."

I waited.

"Then my daughter died."

"I don't understand," I said. "Did your husband die from poison?"

She shook her head.

"No. From a heart attack."

I didn't get it.

I looked at Violet.

"There was so much loss for me. One right

after the other. I was distraught."

"I don't know what you're getting at," I told Violet.

She looked confused.

"My granddaughter. She started coughing," Violet said.

"Coughing?" I asked.

"Non stop," she said quietly. "The poor baby died shortly after that."

"Of cancer?" I asked.

"I thought it was cancer," she said. "Just like my daughter."

I nodded.

Tears welled up in my eyes.

"I guess she did too," Violet whispered.

I nodded again. Wiped at my eyes.

"But the doctor said it was only bronchitis."

I was shocked.

"*Bronchitis?*" I said a little too loudly.

"Yes. And not a very bad case of it, either. The doctor said… she shouldn't have died."

My heart sank.

Poison, Anyone?

I could taste bile in my mouth.

"Are you thinking what I'm thinking?" she asked me.

I was thinking about the poison. The vial of poison.

I wondered.

My mind was spinning with thoughts.

"Tell me about the poison," I said.

"My husband had a theory. There are many children with autism. Too many."

"And?" I asked.

"And. Well. Do you know what pressure treated wood is?"

That threw me for a loop.

"You mean the wood they use for patios?" I asked.

"Yes," she said. "Do you know they use arsenic to treat the wood?"

"*Arsenic*?" I asked. "No. I didn't know that."

"They do," she said simply. "My husband leached that arsenic from some wood. Wood used to make the back patio of a nearby family. A family with a young boy. A boy who was severely autistic."

I stared at Violet.

"The boy was fine until he was two. Then the autism kicked in."

"Did he play on their back patio?" I asked.

"All the time," she said softly.

I was shocked.

"My husband wanted to prove that it was the wood patio. Made with pressure treated wood. He believed that that *wood* made their son autistic. Well, the arsenic in the wood. But... he died before he could prove anything."

"What happened to his research?" I asked.

I was thinking about that vial of arsenic.

The poison he'd extracted from the wood.

"I never touched a thing. Far as I know? It's still in his workshop. In the garage."

Her face was stark white.

"That's what I'm wondering," she said.

"What?" I asked.

"My granddaughter. She thought she had

Poison, Anyone?

cancer. Like her mother."

Oh, my God. I got it now.

"And she saw her mother's painful death," I added.

Could the girl have possibly done what I was thinking?

What Violet was thinking?

I looked at Violet.

"Do you think she did it?" Violet asked aloud.

She sobbed loudly.

I didn't know.

I couldn't answer.

I didn't think it was my place.

I also didn't want to say it out loud.

"If she did it?" Violet said. "Then that selfish, no good, mean man…"

She couldn't finish her sentence.

But I was so angry, I could.

"That selfish no good man *killed* her!"

Her eyes closed slowly.

"Yes. He killed my baby. *And* my grandbaby."

Tears flowed down her wrinkled cheeks freely.

Chapter 18

I let her have some time.

This needed to sink in.

We both sat and cried.

I admit it. I cried.

I cried for the old woman.

I cried for her daughter.

I cried for her granddaughter.

I cried for the tragic waste. The waste of a young life. Two young lives, really.

"I should hate him," she said softly.

I would understand if she did.

"But it won't bring them back," she added.

I wiped my eyes.

"No. It won't," I agreed. "But…" I started to

say.

She cut me off.

"But it will only hurt *me*. Not him. Me."

She had a point.

"And he's hurt me enough already," she whispered.

I nodded slowly.

"He's hurt me enough for three lifetimes."

I looked at Violet. Before? I'd seen a frail old woman.

I had misjudged her.

She was not frail.

She was strong.

Stronger than I. Stronger than anyone I knew.

I could learn a lot from this woman.

"Oh," she said. "Don't get me wrong. I don't forgive him."

I was confused.

"But I won't give him the power to hurt me once more."

I watched her closely.

"And I won't let him sap me of my strength,"

she added.

She was amazing,

Truly amazing.

"I will go on," she said. "I will live my life for all three generations."

She rose from the couch.

She stretched herself up to her tiny height.

She straightened her bent frame as best she could.

She looked right at me.

Head on.

"How about that tea now, Dan?" she asked proudly.

"I'd love some, Violet," I replied.

Now that Dan has solved *this* problem, read the next **JUNKYARD DAN** book **A PICTURE TELLS A THOUSAND DOLLARS** to find out about that micro media card Bubba found in one of Dan's vehicles. What was on that card? What could it be? If Bubba couldn't discuss it? It *had* to be bad. *Very* bad. Find out by reading the *next* book in the series!

Want to read more
JUNKYARD DAN
books?

Go online to
www.NoxPress.com
to see what's being released!

Books can easily be purchased online
or you can contact **Nox Press**
via the Website for quantity discounts.

Are you a fan?
Do you want us to put *your* comments
up on our Website?
If so, please e-mail them to:
NoxPress@gmail.com

NOX PRESS
books for that extra kick to give you more power

www.NoxPress.com